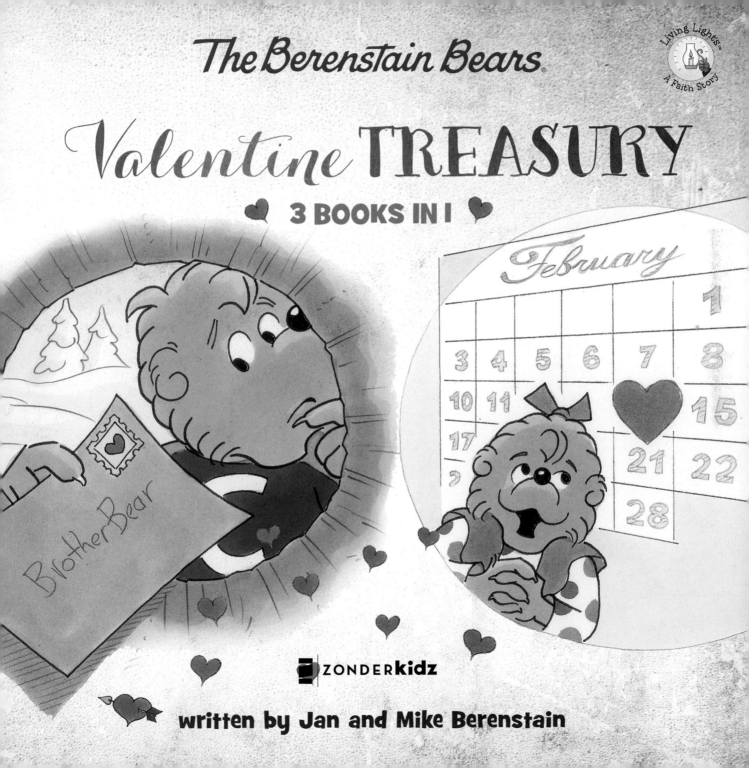

"Dear friends, let us love one another,
for love comes from God."
—1 John 4:7

ZONDERKIDZ

The Berenstain Bears® Valentine Treasury
Copyright © 2019 by Berenstain Publishing, Inc.
Illustrations © 2019 by Berenstain Publishing, Inc.

ISBN: 978-0-310-63121-7

Requests for information should be addressed to:
Zonderkidz, 3900 *Sparks Drive SE, Grand Rapids, Michigan* 49546

The Berenstain Bears® Valentine Blessings
Copyright © 2013 by Berenstain Publishing, Inc.
Illustrations © 2013 by Berenstain Publishing, Inc.

The Berenstain Bears® Love Thy Neighbor
Copyright ©2009 by Berenstain Publishing, Inc.
Illustrations ©2009 by Berenstain Publishing, Inc.

The Berenstain Bears® Bedtime Blessings
Copyright ©2017 by Berenstain Publishing, Inc.
Illustrations ©2017 by Berenstain Publishing, Inc.

All Scripture quotations, unless otherwise indicated, are taken from The
Holy Bible, New International Version®, NIV®. Copyright © 1973, 1978, 1984,
2011 by Biblica, Inc.® Used by permission. All rights reserved worldwide.

Printed in China

18 19 20 21 22 23 / DSC / 6 5 4 3 2 1

When winter comes to Bear Country, a young cub's mind usually turns to thoughts of ice hockey. And Brother Bear was no exception. He was the star forward of his hockey team, the Bear Country Cousins. The big game with their crosstown rivals, the Beartown Bullies, was coming soon. In fact, it was set for Valentine's Day, February 14th. Brother and his whole team were practicing hard every afternoon.

The day before the big game, Brother came home from practice still thinking about his slap shot. He looked in the mailbox and saw a big pink envelope addressed to him. Still thinking about hockey, he opened it. To his shock, it was a big, pink valentine!

It said:

"Oh, Brother Bear,
Will you be mine?
From, Sweetie Bear—
Your Supersecret
Valentine."

"Sweetie Bear?" Brother gasped. "Who on earth is that? Who could have sent this card to me?"

Sister Bear noticed Brother's stunned look as he came inside. And she noticed the big pink envelope in his hand.

"What's that?" she asked. "Looks like a valentine!"

"Oh, it's nothing," said Brother, hiding the valentine behind his back.

But Sister wasn't fooled. She wasn't very interested in ice hockey. But she sure was interested in Valentine's Day. All those hearts and flowers were right up her alley. It looked to her as though Brother Bear had a secret admirer.

"How's the ice, Brother?" asked Papa.

"Ice?" said Brother, still thinking about the valentine. "What ice?"

"The ice for the hockey game!" said Papa. "Is it going to be okay for the big game?"

"Oh, sure," said Brother. "It'll be fine."

"What's the matter, son?" Papa asked. "Are you worried about the game? Those Bullies are a pretty tough team."

"Oh no," said Brother. "It's not that. It's just …" He shrugged and showed Papa the valentine.

Papa looked at the valentine and smiled.

"I know how you feel," he said. "I got a valentine like this when I was about your age."

"At first, I worried a lot," said Papa. "It was from a secret admirer who just called herself Cutie Bear."

"Yuck!" said Brother.

"Just what I said myself," agreed Papa. "I wondered who it could be from. Then it hit me. It must be that cute girl cub who sat next to me in school. She was always giggling and smiling at me."

"Gosh!" said Brother. "What did you do then?"

"Do?" said Papa. "Why, I up and married the girl!"

Brother's mouth dropped open.

"You … married her?" he said.

"Not back then," said Papa, laughing. "I married her later on. It was your mother!"

"Mama Bear?" said Brother taking it all in.

"That's right, son." Papa smiled. "After all, it had to start sometime."

Brother thought that over a little. "Double yuck!" he whispered to himself.

"Don't worry about this Sweetie Bear," said Papa, patting Brother's shoulder. "I'm sure whoever she is she must be a very nice girl. She just has a big crush on a handsome young hockey player."

Brother blushed.

"And remember," Papa went on, "having a crush is nothing to be ashamed about. All love comes from God. As the Bible says:

'Love is patient, love is kind. It does not envy, it does not boast, it is not proud … Love never fails.'"

Brother had never thought about it that way before. Talking to Papa made him feel better about the whole thing. Now he could concentrate on what was really important—hockey!

The day of the big game—Valentine's Day—arrived at last. Brother suited up in his hockey gear. His whole family and lots of other folks from Bear Country went down to the frozen pond to watch the game.

Brother joined his team to warm up. The Beartown Bullies warmed up on the other side of the pond. They were big and tough—especially their goalie. Whoever was under that scary-looking goalie's mask was one terrific hockey player.

The referee dropped the puck and the game was under way. The Bullies were tough opponents, indeed. But the Country Cousins knew their stuff, too. The game seesawed back and forth. Finally the score was two to two with only a few seconds left on the clock. Brother drove for the Bullies' net. He took a hard check and sprawled on the ice. As he fell, his stick slapped the puck which slipped into the Bullies' net right under the goalie's guard. The game was over and the Country Cousins were the winners, three to two!

The crowd cheered long and loud. Brother noticed that some of the cute girl cubs from school were cheering louder than anyone. In fact, some of them were cheering about … him!

"Brother, Brother—like no other! Yay, Brother!" they chanted.

Brother wondered if one of them might be his secret admirer, Sweetie Bear.

The two teams lined up to shake hands after the game. When Brother came to the Bullies' goalie he had quite a surprise. She—that's right—she had taken off her mask. The Bullies' big, rough, tough goalie was a she! It said so right there, on the extra-large T-shirt of Miss Sweetie Bear.

"Sweetie Bear is you?" asked Brother.

"Yes indeed-y," said Sweetie Bear. "I really admire the way you skate. Maybe we could practice together sometime."

"Sure," he said. "Why not?"

Sister was very pleased with how things turned out. She skated around Brother and Sweetie Bear thinking about little hearts and flowers.

"Sister!" said Brother, angrily.

"Now Brother," Mama said. "It's Valentine's Day. Besides, let's remember what the Bible says: 'Anyone who loves God must also love their brother and sister.'"

"I love you, Brother dear!" said Sister.

Brother rolled his eyes. "I love you too, Sis," he sighed.

After all, it was Valentine's Day.

The Berenstain Bears

Love Their Neighbors

written by Jan and Mike Berenstain

ZONDERkidz

Living Lights™
A Faith Story

The Bear family was quite proud of their handsome tree house home, and they worked hard to keep it neat and tidy. The trim was freshly painted, the front steps were scrubbed, and the windows were washed. The lawn was mowed, and the flower beds were weeded. Even the leaves of the tree were carefully trimmed and clipped.

Most of their neighbors took good care of their homes as well. The Pandas across the street were even bigger neatniks than the Bears. It seemed they were always hard at work sweeping and cleaning.

Farmer Ben's farm just down the road was always in apple-pie order too. Even his chicken coop was as neat as a pin. "A place for everything and everything in its place, that's my motto," said Farmer Ben.

The Bear family had a few neighbors whose houses were positively fancy—like Mayor Honeypot, the bear who rode around Bear Town in his long lavender limousine. His house was three stories tall and built of brick. It had a big brass knocker on the front door and statues of flamingos on the front lawn.

Even more impressive was the mansion of Squire Grizzly, the richest bear in all Bear Country. It stood on a hill surrounded by acres of lawns and gardens. Dozens of servants and gardeners took care of the place.

The Bear family was proud of their neighborhood, and they got along well with all their neighbors.

Except for the Bogg brothers.

The Bogg brothers lived in a run-down old shack not far from the Bear family's tree house—but what a difference! Their roof was caving in, and the whole place leaned to one side. There was junk all over the yard. Chickens, dogs, and cats ran everywhere. A big pig wallowed in the mud out back.

"Those Bogg brothers!" Mama would say whenever she saw them. "They're a disgrace to the neighborhood!"

"Yes," agreed Papa. "They certainly are a problem."

One bright spring morning, the Bear family was working outside, cleaning up and fixing up, when the Bogg brothers came along. They were driving their broken-down old jalopy. It made a terrific clanking racket.

The Bears

As they drove past the tree house, one of the Bogg brothers spit out of the car. It narrowly missed the Bears' mailbox.

"Really!" said Mama, shocked. "Those Bogg brothers are a disgrace!"

"I agree," said Papa, getting the mail out of the mailbox. "I'm afraid they're not very good neighbors."

Papa looked through the mail and found a big yellow flier
rolled up. He opened it and showed it to the rest of the family.

"Oh, boy!" said Sister and Brother. "It's like a big block party! Can we go?"
"It certainly sounds like fun," said Mama. "What do you think, Papa?"
"Everyone in town will be there," said Papa. "We ought to go too."
"Yea!" cried the cubs.

So, on Saturday morning, they all piled into the car. They had a picnic basket and folding chairs. They were looking forward to a day of fun and excitement.

But, as they drove along, the car began to make a funny sound. It started out as a Pocket-pocketa-pocketa! But it soon developed into a Pocketa-WHEEZE! Pocketa-WHEEZE!

"Oh, dear!" said Mama. "What is that awful sound the car is making?"
Just then, the car made a much worse sound—a loud CLUNK! It came
to a sudden halt, and the radiator cap blew off. They all climbed out, and
Papa opened the hood.

"I guess it's overheated," said Papa, waving at the cloud of steam with his hat.

"Oh, no!" said Sister. "How are we going to get to the Bear Town Festival?"

"Maybe someone will stop and give us a hand," said Papa hopefully. "Look, here comes a car. Let's all wave. Maybe they will stop."

It was Mayor and Mrs. Honeypot in their long lavender limousine. They were on their way to the festival too. Their car slowed down, but it didn't stop. The mayor leaned his head out of the window.

"Sorry, we can't stop!" he said. "We're late already. I'm Master of Ceremonies today. I've got to be there on time. I'm sure someone will stop to help you."

And he pulled away with a squeal of tires.

"Hmm!" said Papa. "Maybe someone else will come along."

Soon, another car did come along. It was Squire and Lady Grizzly
being driven to the festival in their big black Grizz-Royce. They slowed
down too. Lady Grizzly rolled down her window.

"I'm afraid we can't stop," she said. "We don't have time. I am the
judge of the flower-arranging contest. We simply must hurry."

And with that, they pulled away.

"Maybe no one is going to stop," said Sister. "Maybe we're never going to get to the festival."

"One of our neighbors is sure to stop and help us," said Mama. "After all, that's what neighbors are for."

"Yeah," said Brother. "But do *they* know that?"

A cloud of dust appeared down the road.

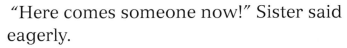

"Here comes someone now!" Sister said eagerly.

The dust cloud drew closer, and they could hear a clackety racket getting louder.

"Uh-oh!" said Papa, shading his eyes and peering down the road. "If that's who I think it is …"

It was!

It was the Bogg brothers.

They came clanking up in their rickety old jalopy and screeched to a halt. First one, then another, then another of the Bogg brothers came climbing out.

"Howdy!" said the first Bogg brother.

"Hello, there," said Papa.

"I'm Lem," said the first Bogg brother. "I can see yer havin' some trouble with your ve-hicle."

"Well, yes, we are," said Papa.

"Maybe we can give you a hand," said Lem.

"That would be very neighborly of you," said Papa.

"Hey, Clem! Hey, Shem!" called Lem. "Git out the rope!"

The other two Bogg brothers rooted around in the back of the jalopy and came up with a length of rope. They hitched it to the back bumper of their car and tied the other end around the front bumper of the Bears' car.

"All aboard!" said Lem. The Bear family climbed hastily back in their car. The Bogg brothers pulled away, towing the Bears' car behind them.

"Where are they taking us?" asked Mama.

Papa shrugged. "At least we're moving!"

Brother and Sister hoped the Bogg brothers weren't taking them down to their old shack. They didn't want to meet that big pig.

They soon pulled into a run-down old filling station. Someone who looked like an older version of the Bogg brothers came out.

"Hello, Uncle Zeke," said Lem.

"Hello, Nephew," said Uncle Zeke. "What can I do you fer?"

"These poor folks broke down on the road," said Lem. "You reckon you can fix them up?"

"Let's take a look," said Uncle Zeke.

He looked under the car's hood, banged and clanged around, and came up with a length of burst hose.

"Radee-ator hose," he said. "Busted clean open. I should have another one of them around here somewheres."

Uncle Zeke rummaged around behind the filling station and soon came back with a radiator hose. He banged and clanged under the hood for a few more minutes.

"There," he said, wiping his hands. "Good as new. We'll top off the radee-ator, and you folks can be on your way."

"Thank you very much!" said Papa, relieved. He shook hands with Uncle Zeke and the Bogg brothers.

"Thank you!" said Mama, Brother, and Sister. Honey Bear waved. "How much do we owe you?" asked Papa, reaching for his wallet. "Nothin'," said Lem. "This one is on us. After all, we're neighbors."

"That's right," said Mama with a gulp. "We are. In fact, how would you neighbors like to come over to our house for dinner next week?"
Papa, Brother, and Sister all stared at Mama with their mouths open.

"That's right neighborly of you," said Lem. "Don't mind if we do! Shem's cookin' has been getting a bit tiresome—too much possum stew."

"We were on our way to the Bear Town Festival," said Papa. "Would you like to join us?"

"Sure would!" said Lem. "We ain't been to a big shindig since Grandpap's ninetieth birthday party!"

So, the Bear family drove to Bear Town with the Bogg brothers and Uncle Zeke.

They were a little late, but they hadn't missed much …
just Mayor Honeypot's welcoming speech. They all joined in
the games, rides, and contests.

When it was time for the fireworks, the Bogg brothers livened things up with some music of their own.

The next week, the Bogg brothers came over to the Bears'
tree house for dinner. They wore their best clothes and
got all spruced up for the occasion. They even brought a
housewarming gift: a big pot of Shem's special possum stew.
It was delicious!

"Love your neighbor as yourself."
"And who is my neighbor?"

—Luke 10:27-29

"In peace I will lie down and sleep,
for you alone, LORD, make me dwell in safety."
—Psalm 4:8

It was evening in the Bear family's tree house. In fact, it was getting late. The sun had gone down long ago, and the western sky was a deep, glowing blue.

Papa was nodding over his fishing magazine. Mama was trying
not to yawn as she worked on a patchwork quilt.

Mama and Papa were growing sleepy, but Brother, Sister, and Honey were still wide-awake. Brother was creating a model of the Mesozoic Age. There were trees and rocks and lots of dinosaurs.

"ROWR! ROWR!" said Brother as he battled a Tyrannosaurus rex against a Triceratops.

Sister was playing with her SuperBear figures. She decided it would be nice if they all had a tea party.

"Would you like another muffin, Mr. Spider Bear?" she asked, politely.

Honey was building a princess castle with blocks. But when it was ready for her princess dolls to move in, she started to feel sleepy. Clearly, she needed something to wake her up.

"Horsey, Papa!" said Honey, hopping onto Papa's lap. "Play horsey!"

"Huh? Wha–?" said Papa, starting out of his doze.

"Horsey! Play horsey!" said Honey.

"Oh!" said Papa, stretching. "Horsey—sure, sweetie-pie. Climb aboard."

Papa boosted Honey onto his back and began galloping around the room.

"Ride 'em, cowboy!" yelled Brother and Sister.

"Now, Honey. Now, Papa," said Mama. "That certainly looks like fun. But it's time to calm down and get ready for bed."

"Bed!" said the cubs. "It's still early! We're not sleepy yet."

"It is not early," said Mama, pointing to the big grandfather clock.

"Tick, tock—tick, tock," said the clock.

"My, my!" said Papa, checking his watch against the clock. "Eight o'clock, already. You're right, my dear, it's time for bed."

"Aww, Mama! Aww, Papa!" said the cubs.

"That's enough of your 'aww-ing'," said Papa. "Come along—up the stairs with you."

With Honey still on his back, he led the way. The cubs were soon in their pajamas with freshly washed faces and teeth thoroughly brushed.

"Story time! Story time!" said the cubs, pulling the big Storybook Bible down from the shelf. They led Papa to his easy chair and climbed onto his lap.

"What story would you like tonight?" asked Papa, opening the Bible. "One with lots of battles and fighting!" said Brother. "Like David and Goliath or Samson and the Philistines."

"How about you, Honey?" asked Papa.

"Bunnies and kitties and lots of animals!" she said, thinking of the story of Noah's Ark.

"And you, Sister?" asked Papa.

"Well," said Sister, thoughtfully. "Sometimes I get bad dreams when bedtime stories are too exciting."

Brother and Honey grew thoughtful. Sometimes they had bad dreams too.

"Are there any Bible stories that will give us sweet dreams?" asked Sister.

"Sweet dreams?" said Papa. "There certainly are. I think I know just the one— the story of Jacob's Dream."

He turned the pages and began to read.

"Jacob was the son of Isaac. Abraham, the first Hebrew, was his grandfather.

One time, Jacob went on a journey. Night came and he grew sleepy. But he had no place to stay. So he lay down on the hard ground with a rock for a pillow."

"While Jacob slept, he had a beautiful dream. He dreamed he saw a stairway reaching from the earth to heaven. The angels of God were going up and down the stairway."

"At the top of the stairway, stood God. He said, 'I am the God of your fathers. I will give your children the land where you lie. They will create a great people who will bless the whole world. I will watch over you wherever you go. I will never leave you.'

"When Jacob woke he knew he was in a blessed place and he promised to serve God all his life."

Papa closed the Bible and kissed Brother, Sister, and Honey goodnight. Mama gently lifted a sleepy Honey into her arms.

"Remember," he said, "God and his angels will always watch over you just as they watched over Jacob."

"That *was* a sweet-dreams story," said Sister, snuggling down and thinking of all those angels. "Goodnight, Papa."

"Goodnight, Papa," said Brother.

"Sweet dreams," Papa said. "God bless you!"

And he turned out the light.

The Berenstain Bears®

9780310712503
$3.99

9780310712497
$3.99

9780310712527
$3.99

9780310712565
$3.99

9780310720898
$3.99

9780310722861
$3.99

9780310720904
$3.99

A Lift the Flap Book
9780310720812
$6.99

A Lift the Flap Book
9780310720836
$6.99

Stickers Included
9780310720850
$4.99

Stickers Included
9780310720881
$4.99

The Berenstain Bears®

Living Lights™
A Faith Story

Bind-ups

5 Books in 1
9780310720102
$10.99

5 Books in 1
9780310725916
$10.99

3 Books in 1
9780310734925
$7.99

3 Books in 1
9780310735038
$7.99

Hardcover Titles

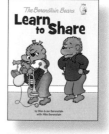

9780310719366
$6.99

9780310719373
$6.99

9780310719380
$6.99

9780310719397
$6.99

9780310722762
$6.99

9780310727149
$6.99

9780310722779
$6.99

9780310727132
$6.99

ZONDERkidz™
.com